Pugicorn

For my family
T.B.

HODDER CHILDREN'S BOOKS

First published in Great Britain in 2019
by Hodder and Stoughton

© Hachette Children's Group, 2019
Illustrations by Tim Budgen

A CIP catalogue record for this book is available from the British Library.

ISBN: 978 1 44495 370 1

5 7 9 10 8 6 4

Printed and bound in China

Hodder Children's Books
An imprint of Hachette Children's Group
Part of Hodder and Stoughton
Carmelite House, 50 Victoria Embankment, London, EC4Y 0DZ

An Hachette UK Company
www.hachette.co.uk
www.hachettechildrens.co.uk

Pugicorn

Written by **Matilda Rose** • Illustrated by **Tim Budgen**

Hodder
Children's
Books

Next time you're in fairyland, make
sure you pay a visit to the Magic Pet Shop
in the town of Twinkleton-Under-Beanstalk.
It's a truly enchanting place.

There are baby dragons, talking llamas,
beautiful phoenixes and even cheeky narwhals.
But the most magical pets of all . . .

. . . are the **unicorns.**
Every year, young princesses and princes
arrive in their carriages to pick a perfect
unicorn pet. This year was no different.

First came Princess Mia.
She chose friendly Flutter Toes.

Prince Alfie chose
shy Glitter Horn,

And Princess Ruby chose
stylish Mellow Curls.

Last to arrive was little Princess Ava. "I'd like a
unicorn, please. With sparkly hooves, a rainbow-coloured
mane and a very, very, very long and swishy tail."

"Dear me!" said Mrs Paws. "It looks like we're all out of
unicorns. But don't worry, I have just the thing . . ."

"Oh!" said Ava. "What is it?"

"It's a pugicorn!" said Mrs Paws.

Pugicorn was small and round, with a funny snuffly
nose, a curly little tail and a rainbow-coloured horn.

Hmm, thought Princess Ava. Pugicorn
wasn't quite what she had in mind.

But Ava had an idea. "Guess what, Pugicorn?
I'm going to turn you into the best unicorn ever.
You'll just need to . . . **Think Unicorn!**"

But Thinking Unicorn didn't help Pugicorn
keep up at the Galloping Gala.

It didn't help him sit still at the Fairies' Garden Party.

Pugicorn definitely wasn't Thinking Unicorn on
his way home from the Mane and Tail Salon . . .

or at Prince Party-Pants' Pet Show.

And as for leaping over rainbows? Nope. No chance.

"You're the worst unicorn ever!"

said Princess Ava. "I'm going to the
Unicorn Picnic and you're not invited."

So Princess Ava stomped off to the Enchanted
Forest, leaving poor Pugicorn all alone.

A little rainbow tear fell down Pugicorn's cheek.
Thinking Unicorn does not come naturally
when you're a pugicorn.

Princess Ava had a wonderful time at the picnic. She ate three delicious confetti cakes and played Unicorn Hoopla. Then Princess Ruby lent her Mellow Curls and together they won the egg-and-horn race.

I wish I had a unicorn . . . not a silly pugicorn, thought Ava, looking longingly at her friends' graceful pets. But the sun was setting and it was almost night. "I think we should go home," said Ruby nervously.

But everything looked different in the dark. Which way was the palace?!

"This way?" said Princess Mia. But Flutter Toes didn't want to get her dainty hooves muddy.

"Down here?" said Prince Alfie. But Glitter Horn refused to tangle her mane on the nasty, prickly branches.

"Through these trees?" suggested Princess Ruby. But an owl hooted loudly above them and Mellow Curls swooned with shock.

You see, unicorns may look dazzlingly beautiful, but they're absolutely no good in a crisis.

Then, just when they thought things couldn't get any worse, the panicking princesses and princes heard a rustling, snuffling sound deep in the forest.

"A MONSTER!" shrieked Princess Ruby.
"What if it eats our confetti cakes?" said Princess Mia.
"What if it eats *us*?" squeaked Prince Alfie.

The sound came closer . . . and closer
. . . and CLOSER, until . . .

"Pugicorn!" gasped Ava.

Her loyal little pet had come to save them,
rainbow lights shining from his magical horn.
A creepy forest was no match for
a plucky little pugicorn!

Together, the princesses, princes and their unicorns
followed Pugicorn as he led them home . . .

. . . squelching – *slip! slop!* – through the mud . . .

. . . stepping carefully over
the prickly bramble bushes . . .

. . . and leaping – *whee!* – across the stream.

Safely back at the palace, Ava gave Pugicorn a tummy-rub, and she even let him chew on her second-favourite slipper.

"I'm sorry I tried to change you," said Ava. "You're not a unicorn. You're a pugicorn – *my* pugicorn – and that's much, *much* better!"

Pugicorn's horn glowed with happiness.

So, everyone in fairyland lived happily ever after:
princesses, princes, pugicorns and not-so-perfect unicorns.

And Mrs Paws' Magic Pet Shop had never been busier.

The most wished-for, longed-for pets in fairyland?

Pugicorns!